MOTHS

ASHLEY GISH

INSECTS X BOOKS

I0809406

CREATIVE EDUCATION · CREATIVE PAPERBACKS

Published by Creative Education and Creative Paperbacks · P.O. Box 227, Mankato, Minnesota 56002 · Creative Education and Creative Paperbacks are imprints of The Creative Company · www.thecreativecompany.us · Design by Rita Marshall · Production by Chelsey Luther · Printed in the United States of America · Photographs by Alamy (Aaron Bastin, Denis Crawford, Jeff Lepore), Dreamstime (Lunamarina, Sander Meertins, Jens Stolt, Tzooka, Unteroffizier), FreeVectorMaps.com, iStockphoto (dalhethe, MindStorm-inc, tshortell, VickieSichau), National Geographic Creative (Robbie George, George Grall, BRECK P. KENT/Animals Animals/Earth Scenes), Shutterstock (Aedka Studio, Robert Biedermann, Coprid, Melinda Fawver, Eric Isselee, Stephen Marques), SuperStock (Biosphoto, NaturePL, Steve Bloom Images)

 • Library of Congress Cataloging-in-Publication Data • Names: Gish, Ashley, author. • Title: Moths / Ashley Gish. • Series: X-Books: Insects. • Includes index. • Summary: A countdown of five of the most fascinating moths provides thrills as readers learn about the biological, social, and hunting characteristics of these hairy, colorful insects. • Identifiers: LCCN 2017060041 / ISBN 978-1-60818-992-2 (hardcover) / ISBN 978-1-62832-619-2 (pbk) / ISBN 978-1-64000-093-3 (eBook) • Subjects: LCSH: Moths—Juvenile literature. • Classification: LCC QL544.2 .G57 2018 / DDC 595.78—dc23

CCSS: RI.3.1-8; RI.4.1-5, 7; RI.5.1-3, 8; RI.6.1-2, 4, 7; RH.6-8.3-8

First Edition HC 9 8 7 6 5 4 3 2 1 • First Edition PBK 9 8 7 6 5 4 3 2 1

MOTH!S

CONTENTS

INSECTS X BOOKS

ANTENNAE
HEAD
WING
THORAX
ABDOMEN

XCEPTIONAL INSECTS

Some moths are big. Others are small. Their bodies and wings have detailed markings. Moths are spectacular colors. They follow an extreme journey from caterpillar to moth.

Moth Basics

Moths are amazing insects. Like all insects, they have six legs and three body parts. All moths have wings, but some cannot fly. Hairy scales cover their body and wings. These scales are **iridescent**. The colors look different depending on how the light hits them.

Moths are different from butterflies. An easy way to tell them apart is their wing posture. Butterflies fold their wings above their bodies while they rest. Moths keep their wings open and out to the sides.

MOTHS OF THE WORLD

There are more than 160,000 kinds of moths worldwide.

MOTHS LIVE EVERYWHERE

in the world except the North and South poles.

MOTH SIZE

Moths vary in size from 0.1 to 12 inches (0.3–30.5 cm) across.

LARGEST MOTH

The largest moth is the Atlas moth from Southeast Asia. Its **wingspan** is 11 inches (27.9 cm). That is wider than a box of cereal!

Compound Eyes

Moths see in all directions.

Moths have compound eyes. These eyes are made up of many parts. They allow a moth to see in many directions at once.

Antennae grow out of moths' heads. Moths use antennae to sense their surroundings. Many have feathery antennae. Some, like the Madagascan sunset moth, have smooth antennae.

Some adult moths have a straw-like mouthpart. This is called a proboscis. It is used to sip **nectar** from flowers. Other adult moths do not have mouthparts. These moths live for only one week. They do not eat.

Many moths have proboscis longer than their bodies.

EXTRA-LONG MOUTHPARTS

Many moths have proboscises longer than their bodies.

MOTH BASICS FACT

Moths use their antennae to smell.

Males can smell females up to seven miles (11.3 km) away!

TOP FIVE XTREME MOTHS

5!

Xtreme Moth #5

Like the Birds Some kinds of sphinx moths in North America are known as hummingbird moths. Hummingbird hawk-moths live in Europe and Asia. Both **species** look and act like hummingbirds. Insects and birds are not related, yet these moths **evolved** to have features similar to hummingbirds. Both moths and hummingbirds needed to sip nectar from long, tubular flowers. So, over time, they developed super-long tongues!

People usually think of moths flying around at night, but many are active during the day.

Moth Babies

Baby moths are called caterpillars. They hatch from eggs. Female moths lay anywhere from 40 to 1,000 eggs. The number of eggs varies by species.

Caterpillars eat leaves. They grow quickly. As they grow, they shed their skin. This is called molting. Many caterpillars eat their molted skin. Within a few weeks, the caterpillars grow big and fat. Then they wrap themselves in a cocoon using silk they produce. Caterpillars stay inside their cocoons for about two weeks.

An extraordinary transformation takes place inside the cocoon. The caterpillar's body begins to change. Its legs and antennae grow longer. Simple eyes become compound. Wings grow from the caterpillar's back. The change from caterpillar to moth takes anywhere from a few days to several months.

When adult moths hatch, their wings are wet. The wings lie close to the moth's body. Moths must rest after hatching. It takes a few hours for their wings to spread out and harden.

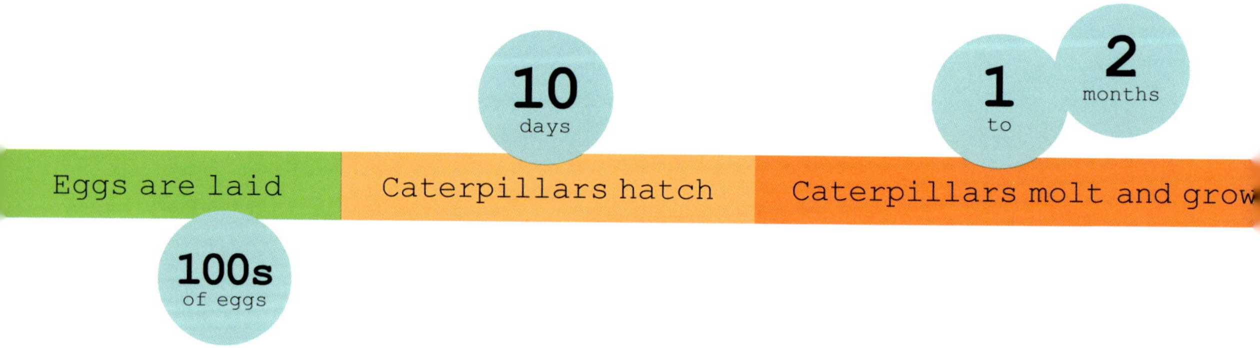

about
2
weeks

surviving
1
week
to
1
year

Caterpillars transform inside cocoons

Moths emerge and mate

MOTH BABIES FACT

Some caterpillars can eat nearly 90,000 times their weight in food in 6 to 7 weeks.

TOP FIVE XTREME MOTHS

4

Xtreme Moth #4

Furry Moths Some moths look fluffy and soft. Rosy maple, silkworm (right), and flannel moths have long scales covering their bodies. The furry scales help them in many ways. They help the moths stay comfortable on hot or cold days. They also provide protection from rain. Flannel moth caterpillars are incredibly hairy. If touched by a predator, the hairs emit a poison. This causes extreme itching and burning.

XTRAORDINARY LIFESTYLE

Moths live short lives. But they play several important roles in nature. To survive, they use poison, **camouflage**, and other features. These help protect them from predators.

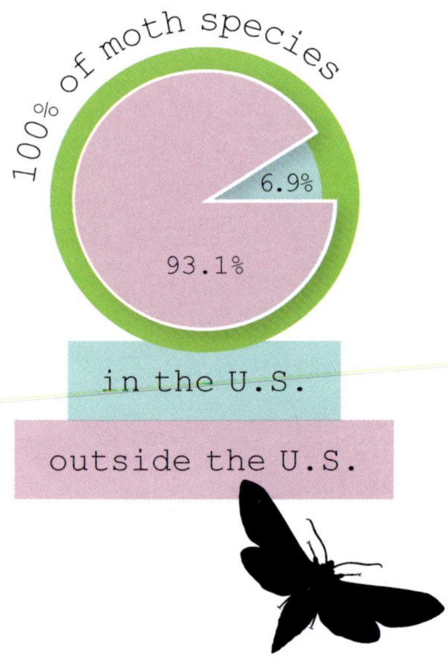

MOTH SOCIETY FACT

Hummingbird hawk-moths fly from southern to northern parts of Europe when the weather warms.

CATERPILLAR X MOLTING

The time between each molt is called an instar.

Moth Society

Unlike many other insects, moths do not usually fly together in groups. Caterpillars that hatch in the same area stay together for a few molts. Eventually, they move away from each other and live alone. Adult moths do not live longer than a year.

Many moths migrate. This means they fly from one place to another, sometimes over many miles. Hummingbird hawk-moths fly from North Africa to Great Britain every summer. This is a journey of more than 2,500 miles (4,023 km)!

Moths make contact only when they search for mates. They do not have noses, but their antennae provide a superior sense of smell. Males can detect females over long distances. Males do not fight each other for the attention of females. Instead, females choose their mates.

XEMPLARY SKILLS

Tiger moths (shown) and hawk moths both make clicking sounds to protect themselves from bats. The sounds disrupt the signals that bats use to locate prey.

XEMPLARY SKILLS FACT

The long tails of luna moths create an echoing sound. This confuses bats that hunt the moths.

Many male moths transfer a defensive toxin to their female mates. The females then become distasteful to spiders. This helps protect the female and her eggs.

Hummingbird moths can hover in the air. They use their long probosces to sip nectar from flowers. As they eat, their bodies pick up pollen. They then carry the pollen to other flowers.

Moths use the moon to fly in a straight line. But when they encounter artificial light, they get confused. This is why moths sometimes fly in circles around a porch light. The moths are too close to the light source. They cannot figure out where to go!

Cinnabar moth caterpillars eat poisonous leaves from ragwort plants. The poison stays in the caterpillars' bodies their entire lives. This makes the caterpillars poisonous, too. They have tiny hairs covering their bodies. These hairs can inject poison into any animal that touches it. The poison is harmful, even to humans. It can cause an itchy rash or make a person feel ill. The caterpillars' bright yellow-and-black coloring warns animals to stay away.

TOP FIVE XTREME MOTHS

Xtreme Moth #3

Scary Eyes North America's polyphemus moth has two dark spots on its lower wings. These spots look like eyes. People used to believe the spots were meant to look like the eyes of a larger animal. In this way, predators would be scared away. But a 2008 study by the University of Cambridge in England suggested something else. The large spots simply startle predators because of their size and color.

XASPERATING CONFLICT

Sometimes moths create conflicts with people. But moths can also be beneficial to the environment. Many animals, such as birds, spiders, frogs, and bats, eat moths and caterpillars.

Moth Survival

Many caterpillars eat crops. Banana moth caterpillars are a problem in Hawaii. They eat the leaves and soft green bark of coffee plants. This kills the plants. Farmers respond to the moth infestations by spraying poison on their plants and planting a variety of crops to confuse the moths.

Some moths are important pollinators. When moths carrying pollen land on other flowers, the flowers can reproduce. Morgan's sphinx moth pollinates orchids. Its proboscis can be a foot and a half (45.7 cm) long!

Moth caterpillars are an important food source for many animals. Every year, songbirds feed their chicks billions of caterpillars. Bats eat moths, too. Moths can be picked off leaves while they are resting.

Some moths look like other animals, such as wasps and tarantulas. This makes them less likely to be eaten.

Brightly colored caterpillars are usually poisonous. **Their** colors are a warning to other animals. **They** warn, "I will make you sick if you eat me!" **Eyespots** are patterns that look like big, fierce eyes. **These** spots are so big and brightly colored that they scare away predators.

MOTH SURVIVAL FACT

The vampire moth has a needle-like proboscis. It drills into animals such as cattle and sucks their blood.

TOP FIVE XTREME MOTHS

2

Xtreme Moth #2

Hidden from Sight Many moths have incredible camouflage. They can be difficult to see. The Pandora sphinx moth is nicknamed the "camo moth." Its color and pattern look like an army uniform. Some Pandora sphinx moths have green camo. They blend in with bushes and leaves. Others have brown or gray camo. These moths blend in with rough tree bark.

XCITING FACTS

The white-lined sphinx moth can fly at speeds of up to 30 miles (48.3 km) per hour.

Metalmark moths protect themselves from jumping spiders by mimicking them.

Every day at Yellowstone National Park, grizzly bears eat up to 40,000 moths!

Some spiders release scents that smell like female moths. Males searching for mates might end up becoming a spider's meal instead.

The mother-of-pearl moth caterpillar defends itself by rolling away from danger at speeds of up to 15 inches (38.1 cm) per second.

The smallest moths are nepticulid moths. They are only 0.1 inch (0.3 cm) across.

The white witch moth has the widest wingspan of any moth: 11.8 inches (30 cm).

In some parts of Africa, people eat caterpillars. They are packed with protein.

Caterpillars' mouthparts have extremely sharp edges for cutting and chewing leaves.

Snowberry clearwing moths are camouflaged to help them look like bumblebees.

The bogong moth used to be a source of food for many of Australia's native peoples.

Cinnabar moth caterpillars can be cannibalistic. That means they eat each other!

In the late 1800s, people

used Madagascan sunset moth (shown)

wings to make jewelry.

TOP FIVE XTREME MOTHS

Xtreme Moth #1

Changing with the Times In the early 1800s, 99 percent of peppered moths were white. They blended in with light-colored plants that grew on trees. But as people built more factories, the plants turned black from factory smoke. Predators could easily see the white moths against the trees. The moths were forced to adapt to their changing world. In about 100 years, after many generations, 90 percent of peppered moths were black!

GLOSSARY

camouflage – the ability to hide by blending in with surroundings

evolved – developed over time from a simple form to a more complex one

iridescent – showing shimmering colors that seem to change when viewed from different angles

nectar – a sugary liquid produced by plants

species – a group of living beings that are closely related

wingspan – the widest measurement across the wings

RESOURCES

Beadle, David, and Seabrooke Leckie. *Peterson Field Guide to Moths of Northeastern North America*. Boston: Houghton Mifflin Harcourt, 2012.

BEAST636. "Evolution of the Peppered Moth." YouTube video, 2:04. Posted February 2009. https://www.youtube.com/watch?v=LyRA807djLc.

"Importance of Moths." Butterfly Conservation. http://www.mothscount.org/text/16/importance_of_moths.html.

"Learn About Butterflies and Moths." The Children's Butterfly Site. http://www.kidsbutterfly.org/faq.

INDEX

Clothes moth caterpillars eat fabric made from wool, silk, and furs